PRAISE FOR *Mom and Dad Are Palindromes*

A Cooperative Children's Book Center (CCBC) Choice of the Year
A *San Francisco Chronicle* Best Children's Picture Book of the Year
A Parents' Choice Awards Silver Honor

"The joke builds nicely, and the illustrations are handsome." —*New York Times Book Review*

★ "Slyly promotes a catchy spelling game." —*Publishers Weekly*, starred review

"Clever." —*School Library Journal*

"Kids will laugh out loud over Robert Trebor's fresh plight. . . . The text crackles with cleverly integrated palindromes." —*Kirkus Reviews*

"The author's nonstop sense of fun and the illustrator's upbeat, comic style breathe energy and interest into an unlikely topic." —Cooperative Children's Book Center (CCBC)

BOB has a problem. He's a palindrome. In fact, as soon as his teacher points out what a palindrome is, Bob realizes there are palindromes everywhere. His PUP OTTO, his little SIS, NAN . . . even MOM and DAD! It's making BOB feel like a KOOK. Is there no escape?

MARK SHULMAN and ADAM McCAULEY have joined forces to create a wonderfully visual, ridiculously clever book of wordplay. Join the hilarity . . . do your civic deed, don't let your pupils slip up, and find the more than 101 palindromes in the words and pictures of this zany book. Fun for home and school. Perfect for readers of *all* ages.

A MAN, A PL...

PASTA, HERO...

COLORATURA

PERCALE, MA...

A BANANA B...

TAG, A BANA...

OR A CAME...

PINS, SPAN, A...

CASH, A JAR,

PEON, A CAN...

N, A CANOE,
S, RAJAHS, A
YAPS, SNIPE,
ARONI, A GAG,
AG, A TAN, A
A BAG AGAIN
E, A CREPE,
RUT, A ROLO,
SORE HATS, A
L—PANAMA!

To Dad, who loved a good word row, born 4-24-24.
And to Hannah, my tot, born in 2002 —M. S.

For Bob and Sös —A. M.

First paperback edition published in 2014 by Chronicle Books LLC.
Originally published in hardcover in 2006 by Chronicle Books LLC.

Library of Congress Cataloging-in-Publication Data available.

ISBN 978-1-4521-3643-1

Manufactured in China.

Book design by Cynthia Wigginton.
Typeset in Ashwood, Gatlin, Matchwood, No. 13 Type,
and Whitecross by Walden Font Co.;
Rosewood by Adobe; and Iceberg by Adam McCauley.
The illustrations in this book were rendered in mixed media.

10 9 8 7 6 5 4 3 2 1

Chronicle Books LLC
680 Second Street
San Francisco, California 94107

Chronicle Books—we see things differently.
Become part of our community at www.chroniclekids.com.

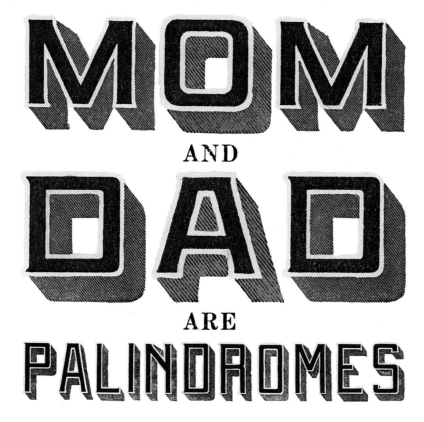

MOM

AND

DAD

ARE

PALINDROMES

A DILEMMA FOR WORDS...AND BACKWARDS

By MARK SHULMAN

Illustrated by ADAM McCAULEY

chronicle books·san francisco

My name is

That might not sound like a problem to you.

But yesterday it almost **DID** me in.

My teacher, **MISS SIM**,

told us about palindromes.

She said:

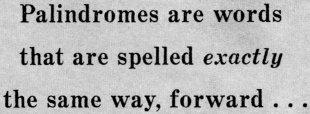

Palindromes are words

that are spelled *exactly*

the same way, forward . . .

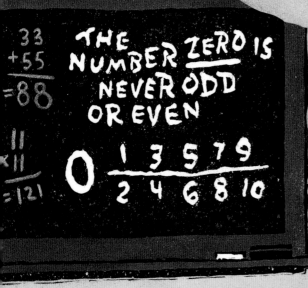

THE
NUMBER ZERO IS
NEVER ODD
OR EVEN

33
+55
=88

11
×11
=121

0 $\frac{1\ 3\ 5\ 7\ 9}{2\ 4\ 6\ 8\ 10}$

AHA!

WHAT A GIG!

TUT, TUT

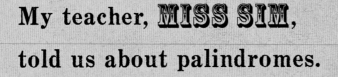

Then she just about
ruined my life.

"We even have a palindrome
right here in class.
Can anyone find him?"

"BOB"

My face became **REDDER** and **REDDER**.

That was just the beginning. Soon it was clear that there were palindromes everywhere.

My **KAYAK**.

My **RACE CAR**.

OTTO, my **PUP**.

. . . and forward.

It was awful.
I needed to tell Mom and Dad and . . . *O NO*!

MOM and DAD

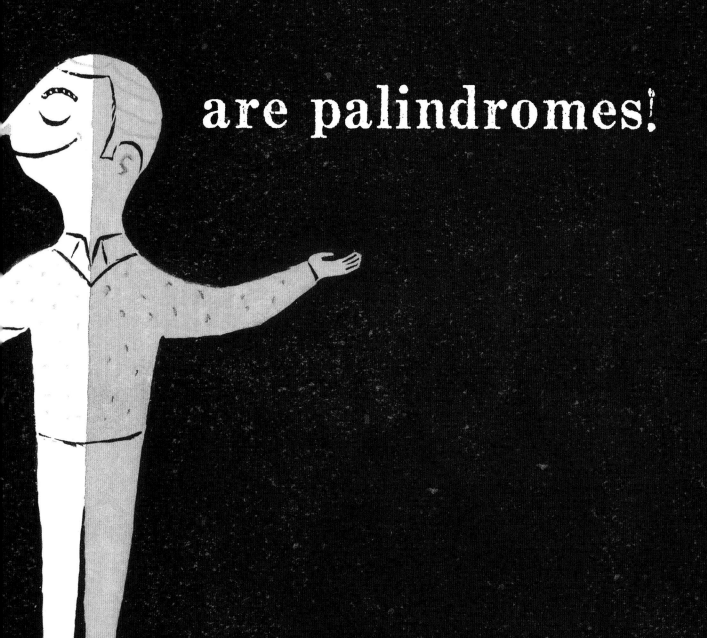

are palindromes!

I ran at **DEEP SPEED** to warn my sister!

Danger, I **SAW, WAS** everywhere. "You're all palindromes!" I yelled. "Even **NAN**! Our little **SIS**! She's just a **TOT**! In a **BIB**! In a **BIRCH CRIB**!"

OO! GOO GOO!

"Maybe a nut," I said,
backing away slowly.

"Maybe a loony. Maybe
even a big fat cuckoo.

But not a

KOOK!"

The clock struck **NOON**. I knew that would happen. Some kids would take the hint. **DID I? I DID**.

I drank some

POP for **PEP**.

It made me **GAG**.

I **DID** a good **DEED** for a **NUN**.
It was a **DUD**.

I tried to run away on a ship.
They had three jobs.

Run the **RADAR**.

Fix the **ROTOR**.

Or **PULL UP**
the anchor.

I left without a PEEP.

Suddenly, a brilliant idea exploded like **TNT**.

"WOW"

Palindromes are really just words and there's more than one way to say any word!

ANNA is really Annabelle!
NAN is Nancy! MOM is
Mother and DAD is Father
and I am Robert! It will get
better, WON'T IT NOW?

I've solved the palindrome puzzle. From now on, I'll only use my full name!

ROBERT

A MAN, A PL

PASTA, HERO

COLORATURA

PERCALE, MA

A BANANA

TAG, A BANA

OR A CAME

PINS, SPAM, A

CASH, A JAR,

PEON, A CAN

N, A CANOE,

S, RAJAHS, A

MAPS, SNIPE,

ARONI, A GAG,

AG, A TAN, A

A BAG AGAIN

L, A CREPE,

RUT, A ROLO,

SORE HATS, A

L-PANAMA!

Also by MARK SHULMAN and ADAM McCAULEY:

"With dynamic layouts on every page, the story is sure to invite rereadings."
—*School Library Journal*

"This tale will surely spark fun wordplay."
—*Kirkus Reviews*

"It is anagram heaven indeed for those who relish such wordplay."
—*Booklist*

MARK SHULMAN has had a mom, a dad, more than one sis, a tot or two (S. S. and Hannah), and a Toyota. He is never odd or even, and between 33 and 44 years old. He is the author of *AA Is for Aardvark, Fillmore & Geary Take Off!*, and more than 55 other books for children and adults. He comes from Rochester, Buffalo, and now New York, NY. And yes, his office address is a palindrome, too.

"Madam, I'm ADAM" McCAULEY is the author and illustrator of *My Friend Chicken*. He has also illustrated many other picture books and chapter books for children, including The Time Warp Trio series and *Sideways Stories from Wayside School*.